BEASTS
–OF–
OLYMPUS

To all my lovely American readers,
with thanks from me and Demon.

GROSSET & DUNLAP
Penguin Young Readers Group
An Imprint of Penguin Random House LLC

Text copyright © 2016 by Lucy Coats. Illustrations copyright © 2016 by Brett Bean. All rights reserved.
Published by Grosset & Dunlap, an imprint of Penguin Random House LLC, 345 Hudson Street, New York,
New York 10014. GROSSET & DUNLAP is a trademark of Penguin Random House LLC.
Printed in the USA.

Library of Congress Cataloging-in-Publication Data is available.

ISBN 978-1-101-99505-1   10 9 8 7 6 5 4 3 2 1

BEASTS
—OF—
OLYMPUS

by Lucy Coats   art by Brett Bean

Centaur School

GROSSET & DUNLAP
An Imprint of Penguin Random House

CHAPTER 1

ITCHY GRIFFIN

Since the Colchian Dragon had nearly exploded Olympus, Demon had learned oodles and squoodles of useful stuff about mixing medicines and proper animal doctoring from his centaur teacher, Chiron. There was one thing, however, he just couldn't seem to get right.

"AARRRGGHH!" The official stable boy to the gods and apprentice healer stood up, threw down the slate he was writing on, and stamped on it. Twice. He looked at the book that lay open beside him on the bale of silver hay. The letters next to the beautiful pictures on the pages were all wriggly and squirrelly and squiggly. His own attempts to copy them were even worse. "I'm NEVER going to learn to write properly," he said, sitting down again with a despairing thump.

A large beak reached down from the roof of the Stables of the Gods and nipped his ear.

"What's up, Pan's scrawny kid?" asked the griffin, flapping down through the light of another bright Olympus day. "Why the long face? You look as grumpy as the giant scorpion." It sat its lion's rump down and began to scratch under its wing feathers with a sharp-clawed back paw.

"Chiron says I have to make notes on all my new patients now," Demon replied. "But the letters won't stay still. They all wiggle and try to run away when I read them, AND when I write them down. It's giving me a headache as big as a hill."

The griffin scratched some more. "Sounds like a puzzle for old Heffy to me," it said. "Why not go on up to the forge and ask him what to do about it?"

Demon looked around him. He'd worked extra hard to get the Stables spick-and-span that morning. All the immortal beasts were clean and munching on ambrosia cake or sun hay. He wasn't due down at Chiron the centaur's cave for his lesson till later.

"Good idea," he said. Then he frowned at the griffin. "Stop scratching. You'll make yourself bleed." But the beast just turned its eagle head around and used the pointy tip of its beak to scratch even harder.

"I've got an itch," it said sulkily. "Not that you care, running off to earth all the time like you do now."

Demon rolled his eyes. "I'll ask Chiron what ointment to mix up for you," he said.

"Why not ask that magic medicine box of yours?" the griffin asked. "No need to trouble your teacher."

Demon sighed. "I can't," he said. "Chiron's forbidden it to help me anymore—at least till I've learned much more about proper healing. But he's already taught me loads and loads of things, so don't worry. I'll bring something back with me tonight."

"You'd better," said the griffin, swishing its tail. "Or else."

As Demon set off up the mountain, his book under one arm, to visit the smith god, Hephaestus, he wondered nervously what the griffin's "or else" might mean. He'd been on the wrong side of a few griffin wounds by now—and they hurt.

A long arrow-pointed tail, covered in bright purple

scales, snaked out of the smith god's cave. Demon stepped carefully around it and poked his head through the door.

Hephaestus was standing by the Colchian Dragon, scratching it behind the horns with his grimy fingers. The dragon's eyes were closed in bliss, and happy orangey-purple jewel tears were rolling down its face, dropping with tiny plinks onto the dirty floor, where they shone like miniature stars.

"Good dragon," said the smith god encouragingly. "Just a few more and I'll have enough for Hera's new tiara. Then you can have as much charcoal as you can eat."

Demon eyed the dragon's bulk. If it ate much more charcoal, he reckoned Hephaestus would have to get a bigger cave. But he wasn't going to suggest that the beast go on a diet. The memory of its terrible farting problem and how it had nearly blown up the whole of Olympus was still too fresh in his memory. Just then, Hephaestus turned around and saw him.

"Hello, young Pandemonius! What's up?"

After Demon had explained, the smith god tapped one grubby fingernail against his teeth, thinking. "Young Eros had just the same trouble," he said. "Aphrodite kept after me for months to sort him out after he wrote some love letters all wrong and nearly started a war." He chuckled. "He's a little scamp, is Eros. Him and his love potions. Always some poor girl or boy with hearts coming out of their ears." He went over to a wooden box, rummaged around, and came out holding some thick golden wire and some dusty square blocks of blue, pink, and yellow crystal, which he cleaned off with a damp rag.

"What are those for?" Demon asked. Behind him, the chubby dragon made loud, happy crunching sounds as it munched on a trough full of charcoal.

"You'll see," said Hephaestus, setting them down on his workbench. Working fast, he twisted and turned the wire in his big, grimy hands until he had a strange-looking frame with two attached circles and two long arms. Then he carefully tapped each block of crystal with a small silver hammer until he had three thin, transparent sheets of different colors. He beckoned to Demon. "Give me the book." Demon handed it over, and quickly the smith god set it open and laid a sheet of blue crystal over it. "Have a look," he ordered.

Demon looked. The letters were just as squiggly as ever. He shook his head. Hephaestus whipped away the blue crystal and replaced it with the yellow. Demon shook his head again. Yellow made his stomach want to heave.

"I don't think it's working," he said. A little knot

of despair was growing inside him. If the letters didn't behave, he'd never be able to be a proper apprentice healer to Chiron.

"Don't give up yet, boy," said the smith god. He laid down the pink crystal, and suddenly, everything on the page was still and clear.

"Oh!" said Demon, staring at the straight, elegant lines of writing. "It's like magic!"

"Not magic this time," said Hephaestus, looking smug underneath his huge black beard. "Just godly cleverness." He took one of the dragon's jewel tears and used its sharp point to cut two little circles out of the pink crystal, fixing them tightly within the circles on the golden frame. Then he popped them on Demon's nose and fastened the arms behind his ears. After making a few adjustments, he stood back.

"There you are," he said. "Problem solved! I call them opticles."

With the opticles on, Demon's world was now slightly pink tinted, but he didn't care. Now he could take proper notes! Chiron would be happy.

Demon got off the Iris Express rainbow and went into the light, airy cave to find his teacher. Neither Chiron, nor his assistant, Asclepius, was anywhere to be seen. However, Demon could hear a strange noise in the distance, a sort of snorty, shouty sound and some high screaming. Maybe an animal was in trouble, and the centaur god had gone to heal it. He ran outside to see.

At first there was nothing, only the usual silvery cistus shrubs and olive trees waving in the breeze with the watery blue of King Poseidon's realm down below. But then, from around the corner, came a tall, thin young man. He ran so fast that he was past Demon and into the cave before Demon could do more than gasp. Behind the young man, in a cloud of white dust, galloped a crowd of about twenty centaurs. These weren't nice calm centaurs like Chiron. Oh no! These were angry centaurs, with rolling red eyes and bared white teeth and rearing hooves that pounded the ground so hard that it shook.

Demon threw himself into a bush just in time, as a plate-size hoof slapped through the air exactly where his head had been.

"Whoa!" he said breathlessly, heart thumping harder than a hammer on an anvil. "What's going on?" But nobody heard him. The herd of centaurs milled around in front of the cave, stamping angrily and swishing their tails like vicious fly swatters. In their hands he could see torn-off tree branches and slings full of rocks.

"Peleus!" they screamed. "Prince Peleus! Come out and die!"

Demon eyed the angry mob. Things weren't

looking too good for this Prince Peleus, whoever he was. "Suppose I'd better go and help," he muttered, pushing the bag that held his book and the precious opticles into the space between two rocks.

He crawled through the bushes on his belly to avoid being seen, slipped around the side of the mountain, and climbed into Chiron's cave by a back window. As he landed, a body shot out from under one of the empty beds and tackled him to the ground, pinning his arms over his head with two strong hands.

"Oof!" Demon grunted. "Get off me! I've come to help!"

Two very green eyes looked at him down a long, thin nose, before letting him up.

"Bit small for a warrior, aren't you?" said Prince Peleus scornfully, flicking back his straight black hair. "Where's your sword? You can't stab those centaurs without a sword."

Demon dusted himself off before replying. He was fed up with people thinking that everything could be sorted out with swords and violence.

"I'm not a warrior," he said. "And I don't need a sword." Without another word, he marched to the front of the cave and pulled out his father's silver pipes from the front of his tunic. Putting them to his lips, he blew a long, discordant blast that echoed off the rocks, bouncing back and forth like shrill thunder.

"Hey!" he shouted. "Shut up and listen."

It was as if a sheet of perfect silence had fallen over the mountain. Not a bird sang, not a cricket chirped.

Then the lead centaur snorted, red foam dripping from his lips. "Who are you, boy? And what are you doing with Pan's pipes? Just wait till he catches you! He'll tear you apart with his teeth."

"Pan's my dad," said Demon. "And he gave them to me, so there. Now, what do you want with Prince Peleus?"

As if the name had lit a fire under them, the centaurs began to scream and rear and shout again. Demon was just about to blow his dad's pipes once more when a great voice shouted from the back of the herd.

"STOP THAT RACKET AT ONCE!"

The centaurs all wheeled around and fell to their knees.

Chiron the centaur god had arrived.

CHAPTER 2
THE LOST SWORD

Demon watched admiringly as Chiron sent the
centaur herd trotting away after giving them a good
telling-off for daring to trespass on his mountain.
He didn't allow them to say a single thing other
than "yes, Chiron," "no, Chiron," and "sorry,
Chiron." By the time he had finished with them,
their heads were low, and their tails were drooping.
Then he turned to Demon, tossing him a large sack
full of strong-smelling herbs.

"By Zeus's toenails, young Pandemonius! What's

been happening around here?"

Demon caught the sack, wrinkling his nose and trying not to sneeze. "I don't know. I was just trying to calm them down. They were chasing him." He jerked a thumb over his shoulder at Prince Peleus, who stepped forward from the shadows with a swagger and shouldered his way past Demon to stand in front of the centaur god.

Chiron's bushy eyebrows lowered. "Young Peleus," he growled. "What trouble have you gotten yourself into now, Grandson?"

Peleus shrugged. "I was looking for my sword, Grandpa," he said. "I came up here on a hunting trip with my friend Acastus. But we had a big argument last night. He stole my sword and hid it from me, then he led me into a trap. I didn't know that interrupting a centaur ceremony was such a big thing."

Chiron's brows lowered even farther. "Was there

a big golden bowl involved? And a sheaf of grain?"

Peleus nodded. "I may have knocked over the bowl and scattered the grain when I ran into their glade," he muttered, looking sheepish.

"You were lucky they didn't trample you into tiny little pieces," the centaur god said, snorting.

"Well, I'm sorry," said Peleus, not sounding it at all, Demon thought. "But I had to get my sword back." He stamped his foot. "I HAD to!"

"What's so special about your sword?" Demon asked. "Can't you just get another one? They're all pretty much the same, aren't they?"

Peleus whirled around. "Stupid little boy," he snapped, putting his long nose in the air in a way that made Demon want to give him to the giant scorpion for an afternoon. "Don't you know anything? It's a magic sword. Hermes gave it to me. It makes me invincible in battle."

Suddenly the air grew close and hot, and Demon

felt as if a thousand angry wasps were

buzzing in the air around him and Peleus.

"WHERE ARE YOUR MANNERS,

SON OF MY DAUGHTER?"

Chiron thundered,

in a voice that made it obvious he was Zeus's brother. Then, slightly more quiet, "Pandemonius was brave enough to face down those centaurs for you, young man. Do you really think you should be calling my apprentice healer a 'stupid little boy'?"

Peleus hung his head, blushing. Then he held out a hand to Demon. "Sorry," he said, and this time he sounded like he meant it.

Demon shook it, a warm glow starting somewhere around his heart. Chiron really was on his side, even when the god's own family was involved. It felt good. He was more used to gods threatening to turn him into things—most often a little pile of burnt charcoal.

"Now," said the centaur god, patting Demon on the shoulder. "Come and help me hang the herbs up to dry, both of you, and then we can see about finding this sword."

A few hours later, Demon was beginning to wish he'd let those centaurs have Peleus. Instead of his precious healing lesson with Chiron, he'd been stumbling around all over the mountain with the prince, looking for his wretched magic sword. Listening to the centaur god's grandson boasting about how many soldiers he'd knocked down in his training session and how being a prince was the way to get girls wasn't really Demon's idea of a fun day out. Nor was poking his hands into holes till his fingers were black with dirt, and climbing trees till his knees were skinned and bloody. It wasn't as bad as being bitten by his beasts, but it wasn't far off. Luckily, Offy and Yukus, the golden snakes from his magic necklace, had sorted out the cuts and bruises quite quickly.

"I wonder if I should tell Chiron about you two," he whispered, feeling a bit guilty. "You heard him say I'm not supposed to use magic to heal things anymore."

"We'd advissse ssstaying sssilent," hissed the snakes. "Chiron doesssn't need to know."

"Well, if you really think so," said Demon, peering into yet another rabbit burrow.

"We do," they said, slithering around his neck again and curling their tails together.

By the time they got back to Chiron's cave, both he and Peleus were tired and hungry, and neither of them had found the sword. Demon looked anxiously at the sky. Helios's sun chariot had nearly driven over the horizon. It was time for him to call the Iris Express and go home to Olympus to feed the griffin and the other beasts their evening ambrosia cake.

"Oh no!" he said, smacking himself on the head. "I forgot the griffin's ointment."

"Who?" Peleus asked.

"My . . . I mean . . . Zeus's griffin," he said. "It's got a terrible itch in its feathers, and I was supposed to make something up to cure it today. But with looking for your sword and everything, I haven't exactly had time." He went into the cave to find Chiron. The centaur god was humming to himself as he lit the beeswax candles around his treatment room with a flick of his fingers, making the shadows sway and retreat into the corners.

"Can you tell me what to use for itchy griffin feathers, please?" Demon asked. "We haven't done that lesson yet."

"Itchy griffin feathers? Did you take a proper patient history? Did you write down times and symptoms on your slate like I showed you?"

"No," Demon confessed. "I've had a bit of trouble with the reading and writing. But it's fine now that I've got Hephaestus's opticles," he added hastily.

"Well, go back and do it properly," said his teacher, reaching for a large jar and pouring some dried daisy heads into a little bag. "Meanwhile, crush these up and sprinkle the powder on the itchy bits. It's probably only feather mites. Work it in well with a brush, mind, so it covers the whole area."

"When did the itching start?" Demon asked, the opticles perched on the end of his nose, and his slate propped against his knees. He'd fed all the beasts and cleaned out the Stables as well as pounded the daisy heads to a fine dust, and now he was sitting on the floor in the griffin's pen. It was looking rather sour as it pecked halfheartedly at a large slab of ambrosia cake.

"Dunno," it said. "Yesterday? Day before? Why's it matter, anyway, Pan's scrawny kid?"

"Because Chiron says I have to ask, that's why. Now tell me, what kind of itch is it? Prickly? Hot? Burning?"

"An itchy itch is what it is. Have you got something for it or not? Because if you haven't, I'd appreciate being left alone to eat my dinner and scratch." It picked up the slab in its beak and dropped it on the floor, spraying Demon with small particles of stale ambrosia. "Not that I'm enjoying it tonight. Or any night, really. Disgusting stuff."

Demon sighed. He agreed. Ambrosia was the food of the gods, and it had given him really strong muscles and made him grow much taller since he'd been eating it—but he'd much rather have one of his favorite honey cakes.

"Come on, then," he said. "Spread out your wings. I need to get the powder right into the feathers."

Soon every griffin feather was covered in a grayish-green powder. Demon couldn't see any mites running around, but that didn't mean they weren't there.

"All done," he said, patting the griffin's rough lion pelt. "That should fix it. You'll be fine by the morning."

When Demon crawled out from under his spider-silk blanket at dawn the next day, he whistled happily as he clattered down the ladder. Doris the Hydra was waiting for him with buckets, brooms, and pitchforks dangling from its nine mouths, all ready to help him with his cleaning duties.

"Morning, Doris," he said cheerfully. "Extra snackies if you can help me clean up in double-quick time. I want to get down to Chiron's cave early today." The Hydra fluttered its thirty-six eyelashes and began to drool as Demon fetched the poo barrow. But as he wheeled it up the Stables toward where the Cattle of the Sun were mooing for their breakfast of sun hay, he became aware of a low, angry growling sound coming from the griffin's pen. Cautiously, he unlatched the door and poked his head around it.

At once, a huge, sharp beak lashed out at him, making him jump back and slam the door shut.

"WRETCHED BOY," roared the griffin. "LOOK AT MY FEATHERS!"

Demon stood on tiptoe and peered in cautiously.

The angry beast had retreated to a corner, where it crouched in a huddle, tail lashing furiously. The draft it caused was making a whole pillowful of shed feathers whirl and flutter into the air. The griffin's wings had holes in them, and, almost worse, the tiny golden feathers on its eagle head had fallen off in great clumps, leaving pink bald patches with bright purple spots.

"Oh, *Griffin* . . . ," he began.

But the beast was in no mood for sympathy. "You're going to pay for this, Pan's scrawny kid," it hissed, hurling itself at the bars.

CHAPTER 3

FEATHER DILEMMA

Demon was almost in tears. Had the daisy powder done this? Surely the griffin knew that he'd never hurt a beast deliberately? Nor would Chiron. It was all some terrible mistake, and he needed to fix it. This was an emergency. Chiron wouldn't mind if he used his magic medicine box now. Despite all he'd learned from his centaur teacher, he had no idea what was wrong with the griffin—or how to cure it.

Running like one of Artemis's golden deer, he dashed out of the Stables and over to the hospital shed. His box lay in the corner, its silvery sides looking a little tarnished and dusty. He banged his hand on the lid.

"Wake up, box! The griffin's feathers are falling out. I need you! It's an emergency!"

For a second, his heart leaped as the box glowed blue. But then a big red X flowed over its top and sides.

"Closed for business until further notice," it said in its metallic voice. Then it went dark.

"Nooo!" Demon wailed, running his hands through his hair till it stood on end like a messy brown brush. What was he going to do? He scrabbled through the cupboards, trying to think of something, anything, he could use to help the griffin. Then his hand brushed against something cold—a big copper jar with a stopper.

"Yes!" he whispered. "The ointment I used on King Poseidon's Hippocamps to stop the itchy-scratch." Quickly, he took it down. Feathers weren't that different from scales, were they? Maybe it would help. He opened the jar, then groaned. It was only a quarter full. It would have to do, though. He had nothing else until he could get down to Chiron. Clutching the jar to his chest, he ran back to the Stables.

By this time, all the other beasts were hungry, and clamoring for their morning meal.

"I'm coming! I'm coming!" he called. "But I need to sort out the poor griffin first. Please be quiet—you know how Aphrodite gets if she misses her beauty sleep." As the racket died down a bit, he thought back to the week before and winced. The beautiful goddess had threatened to make him fall in love with the giant scorpion after a particularly loud early-morning bellowing battle between the three fire-breathing bulls. They had had an argument over which one of them was strongest and nearly set the whole Stables on fire.

Demon took a deep breath and went into the griffin's pen. Even more feathers had fallen off it now, and his feet made little swooshing noises as he waded through them. The griffin's eyes were closed, and it was now making distressed little whiffling noises through its beak. As soon as he got close, though, it reared up and tried to scratch him.

"Stop it," he said, dodging the huge claws. "I'm trying to help."

"You'd better, Pan's scrawny kid," it spat. "Or I'll be taking off your fingers and toes one by one. See how you manage then."

By the time he'd finished spreading on the sticky goop, the beast's top half looked more like a bedraggled chicken than a fierce eagle.

"Is it helping the itching?" he asked.

"A bit," it growled. "But you need

to stick my feathers on again, like you did with the winged horses. Or regrow them. I can't go around looking like this. And I can't fly, either. They'll all laugh at me out there, just you wait and see." The griffin looked thoroughly miserable.

"Tell you what," said Demon. "There are some nice airy pens out at the back of the hospital shed. I've never used them, but I think they're meant for any beast who has something the others might catch. Chiron's been teaching me about infections. I don't know if you've got one, but it's best to be safe. You can go in one of those, and no one will be able to see you while you get better."

The griffin looked at him in its usual sly manner. "I'm not hungry at the moment, but I might need a special diet," it said hopefully. "Some nice minced lamb with blood gravy and a sprinkle of scarab beetles. That would make my feathers pop up in no time."

"We'll see," said Demon. "Let's get those purple spots to go away first."

By the time he reached Chiron's cave again, Demon was more tired than a field mouse who'd run a marathon. He'd fed and cleaned in double-quick time, moved the griffin to its new home, and, after washing his hands thoroughly, checked the winged horses and the Caucasian Eagle for any signs of feather-drop and itching. Luckily they all seemed fine.

Chiron was waiting for him, tapping one front hoof impatiently on the ground. "Where have you been? I don't expect my apprentice to be late. It's bad enough that Asclepius has gone off to tend to that new wife of his. I'm snowed under with mortal patients." He frowned down at Demon.

"I-I'm sorry," Demon stammered. "It's my griffin. I don't know what to do . . ." He consulted his slate and read out the griffin's symptoms, then looked up at Chiron. "I'm calling it the Purple Spotted Feather Plague," he said.

"Hmm," said the centaur god. "Purple spots, you say. And extreme feather-drop. Did you say decreased appetite, too?"

Demon nodded. "Do you know what it is, then?" he asked. "What should I treat it with? The griffin threatened to bite off all my fingers and toes if I don't find something quickly."

Chiron gave a sort of strangled cough. Demon looked at him suspiciously. Was his teacher laughing at him? Didn't he realize how serious the situation was? It was no good trying to be a healer with no digits.

"It's definitely an infection, so you did the right thing by isolating the griffin from the other feathered beasts," Chiron said. "You'll need to get anything with feathers away from Olympus, just to be safe. I suggest you tell the Caucasian Eagle to roost in the mountains when he's finished tearing out poor old Prometheus's liver—and I suppose the winged horses can come down here. They'll like a bit of a vacation, I expect."

Demon was still very worried. "It's . . . it's not, well, fatal, is it?" he asked, a big bumpy throat lump making his words hard to get out. He didn't think he could bear it if his friend died.

Chiron laughed out loud this time. "Use that brain of yours, young healer! The griffin's an immortal beast. It might be very sick, but it won't die. The worst that could happen is that Zeus will make it into a set of stars—but he only does that to beasts who've done something to help us gods, not to just an ordinary griffin."

"So what medicine do I use?" Demon asked.

The centaur god shook a green-stained finger at him. "No, no, Pandemonius. I'm not going to tell you what to treat the griffin with. It's time you worked things out by yourself. I'd start by looking up *I* for *Itching* in the big book with the red thread around it." He stamped a hoof and reached for his healer's bag, slinging it over one brown, muscley shoulder. "I'll leave you to it, then, my young apprentice. I'm off to see a patient in the village below—with Asclepius away, I've got more work than I can handle. Why they decided to have a baby, I can't imagine. It's very inconvenient."

Muttering crossly, he trotted off down the mountain, leaving Demon staring after him with his mouth open. He couldn't work out whether he was annoyed at being left, or flattered that Chiron finally trusted him to come up with a remedy all on his own.

He put on his opticles and pulled the book down from the shelf, muttering to himself as he sounded out the difficult words. By the time he'd gotten to the end, he was thoroughly confused. Even with Heffy's invention, he still wasn't very good at reading yet. There seemed to be about a hundred kinds of itching, all with different cures—and none of them was exactly like the griffin's. He went outside to give his brain a rest and bumped straight into a rather bedraggled-looking Prince Peleus, who was sitting on a rock looking very gloomy and picking bits of twig out of his hair.

"Still no luck with the sword?" Demon asked.

Peleus shook his head. "I've looked everywhere," he said. "And I nearly ran into those centaurs again. I had to hide up a tree for ages."

Now that Peleus wasn't boasting, Demon felt a bit sorry for him.

"If you help me look for a cure for my griffin, I'll get all the animals and birds on the mountain to keep an eye out for your sword," he said. "I don't know why I didn't think of it before."

"It's a deal," said Peleus, clapping him so hard on the back that he nearly fell over.

It was so much easier with two people. Peleus wasn't just a boastful warrior. He actually had a brain. The breakthrough came when the prince had the brilliant idea of combining an itching remedy with one for spots. Soon Demon was pounding some sticky white clay with the slimy aloe leaves that grew all over the mountain, a sprinkle of oatmeal, and some dried peppermint. Peppermint seemed to cure almost everything.

"How about some of this?" Peleus suggested, holding out a stone jar he'd taken from Chiron's small, tidy kitchen. Demon took a sniff and choked.

"What's THAT?" he spluttered.

"Spiced apple vinegar. My mom swears by it for bug bites, so it might work for spots."

Demon slopped some in and stirred it around,

then looked at the mixture doubtfully. It had turned out a bit like white porridge, and it smelled funny. He scraped it into a clay jar and sealed it with a bit of waxed parchment and string. He'd get Chiron to check it when he got back.

"Right," said Peleus. "Now where are these animals of yours, young Demon?"

By the time the sun was midway up the sky, Demon had talked to nearly every rabbit, vole, mouse, and chipmunk on the mountain. He'd chatted with lynxes, eagles, and hawks, as well as sparrows, doves, and pigeons. None of them had seen a sword, but they'd all promised to spread the word. He was sitting on a rock, chatting with a crow, when the wolves turned up. Peleus edged behind him.

"Greetings, Pandemonius," the lead wolf said as he and his pack settled in a circle at Demon's feet. Wolves were always rather formal, so Demon bowed.

"Greetings, Father Wolf," he replied. "Do you bring me news of the prince's sword?" The wolf's tail wagged, and his jaws lolled open in a sharp-toothed grin.

"Indeed I do," he said. "Come forth, Little Stinktail, and tell the son of Pan your story."

CHAPTER 4

LITTLE STINKTAIL

A very small female wolf limped forward from the back of the pack. Her fur might once have been white, but now it was covered in smears of brown, and she definitely deserved her name. Demon coughed and tried not to hold his nose. He could hear Peleus choking behind him.

"I was having a nice roll in a big pool of lovely soft cow poo, when something bit me," she whined. "It smelled like old rust and blood, and it was like a big, sharp, pointy tooth. It nearly sliced off my paw."

She held up her front paw, which had a deep cut across the pads. "See?"

"Oh dear," said Demon. "That looks bad. I'd better clean it up and put a bandage on it for you." He looked at Father Wolf. "Would you be prepared to take my friend to where Little Stinktail was wounded?" he asked.

"Most certainly," said Father Wolf. "If he's prepared to run with us, that is." The big animal looked at Peleus and licked his chops.

"Is it thinking of eating me?" Peleus asked, his voice shaking a little. Unlike Demon, he couldn't understand what the wolves were saying.

Demon laughed. The young warrior wasn't so brave now. "Of course not," he said. "Wolves have a great sense of humor. He reckons it's funny to make you nervous. I think they've found your sword, though, so go with them."

Once Peleus had jogged off behind the pack,

Demon turned to Little Stinktail and grabbed her by the scruff of the neck. "You," he said grimly, "are coming with me to the waterfall to get scrubbed."

"What about my poor paw?" Little Stinktail whined.

"Wash first, paw after," Demon said. "You don't want cow poo in your wound—it'll make it go all bad."

The glade by the waterfall was peaceful, and the sun shone through the trees, dappling the grass with spots of greenish gold. By the time Demon had hauled the young wolf into the pool and scrubbed her thoroughly with handfuls of dry leaves, both of them were soaked through and panting.

"Ugh!" he said as he inspected her sore paw. "Now I smell like wet wolf."

"You've washed off all my nice stinky bits," she growled, giving him a little nip and shaking herself so that drops of water flew everywhere, catching the sunlight like tiny round rainbows.

Demon frowned. "None of that," he said. "I'm only trying to help. We'll have to go back to Chiron's cave." He tapped the cut pads gently. "This needs a stitch or two, and a bandage."

But just as they were leaving, someone trotted through the trees toward them. Someone with thick, hairy, goaty legs and big curly horns. Someone with yellow eyes and black, slitty pupils. Someone who wore no clothes and carried a set of silver reed pipes.

Demon dropped to his knees and bowed his head.

"D-Dad . . . I mean, Your Goddishness," he said, trying not to let his voice shake. It was still hard to know what to call a father who was also a god. The wolf dropped to her belly and wriggled forward to Pan's feet, wagging her bedraggled tail frantically.

"Hello, Son," said Pan, bending down

to stroke Little Stinktail before sweeping Demon
up into his arms for a hug.

As usual, he smelled like green things and old blood, and his voice was like mossy velvet caught on crumbly bark. "Got anything for a headache, have you? I've been partying all night with some centaur lads, and I might have had a bit too much of Dionysus's new brew." He put Demon down and rubbed a hand through his wild hair. "Lethal stuff. Take some advice from your old dad—never touch it, however good it smells." Pan sank down on a tree stump, groaning a little. The wolf curled up at his hooves, licking her paw.

Demon looked at his dad. He did look a bit paler than normal. What on Zeus's earth did you give a god for a headache, though? He looked around him, thinking hard, then he saw the willow tree hanging over the pool.

"I've got just the thing," he said, taking out a small, sharp knife from his belt. Whispering thanks to the tree, he shaved off a few thin strips of bark, shredded them, and held them out. "Chew these," he said. "They'll be bitter, but it'll take the pain away."

After making disgusted faces for a few minutes, Pan spat out the chewed bark and sat up, looking a lot brighter. "Clever lad," he said. "You'll be as great a healer as Chiron in no time." Demon glowed with pride. Praise from his dad meant a lot to him, and he didn't often get it.

Pan stretched, the great muscles in his chest rippling. "I must be off again," he said. "But before I go, is there anything I can give you, Son?"

Demon knew he should probably say "nothing," but this was too good a chance to pass up.

"Is there a way I can use your pipes to put just one animal to sleep at a time?" he asked, trying to keep the eagerness out of his voice.

A look of pleased surprise crossed Pan's face. "What? No magic cloak of invisibility or sandals with wings?" he asked. "Not that I'm very good at those, but it's usually what people ask for." Demon shook his head.

"I'm sure they'd be nice, but I'd rather learn to use your pipes properly," he said. "They've been very useful so far."

"Very well, then, my boy." The forest god raised his pipes to his lips. "Look into the beast's eyes and do this." He blew a tricky little low twiddle that raised all the hairs on the back of Demon's neck. Then he played a high, screechy set of notes that made Demon's teeth hurt. "That's the wake-up one, as well, in case you need it. Now you try them."

After Pan had left, Demon practiced all the way back to Chiron's cave until he had the notes just right. Then he looked into Little Stinktail's eyes and put her to sleep while he sewed and bandaged her paw. By the time he'd woken her up again, Chiron was back.

Demon showed him the ointment he and Peleus had made. As the centaur sniffed it and gave Demon an approving nod, Demon thought of something. "How do I get the griffin's feathers back?" he asked. "There are too many of them to stick on, and anyway, I don't think I've got any of the glue left from when Autolykos stole the winged-horse feathers."

Chiron looked at him. "I don't approve of that box of yours normally, but didn't I hear something about you regrowing the feathers on some Stymphalian Birds a while back? You could add a few drops of that medicine to the ointment if you've got any left. Otherwise, I'm afraid it's time and patience." He handed Demon a mask, a bag of pungent herbs, and a huge bottle of green liquid. "Burn all the straw from the griffin's cage, then fumigate the Stables with this sage. Tomorrow at dawn, you must sprinkle the whole place with my patented cleaning liquid. That's when the ingredients are at their strongest. Don't forget now. It's important."

As Demon got off the Iris Express, his head was buzzing with his teacher's instructions. He ran straight to the hospital shed and found the small vial with the feather-regrowing medicine in it. Luckily there were a few drops left. Mixing them into the ointment with a spoon, he walked over to see the griffin.

It was not in a good mood. It was stalking around the cage, growling, and emitting ear-piercingly angry griffin shrieks. Its purple spots were now huge and glowing, and some of the ones on its head had burst in showers of revolting yellow pus that oozed and trickled down its beak.

"YUCK!" said Demon, before he could stop himself. "That's disgusting."

As he put down the ointment and let himself into the cage, the griffin's beak whipped out quicker than a bolt of lightning and snapped off Demon's left little finger, spitting it out immediately.

"I warned you, Pan's scrawny kid! I warned you!" it screamed.

Demon screamed, too. He couldn't help it. The little stump was pouring blood, but there was no time to fix it, because the griffin was coming at him again, going for his bare toes.

Frantically, Demon grabbed his pipes, looked into the raging beast's eyes, and blew Pan's new twiddle. Immediately the beast dropped like a dead thing, slumped on its back with outspread wings and head lolling to the side. Trying not to scream again, Demon fell to his knees, searching for his finger. Was it too late? Had it been burned up by toxic griffin spit? No, there it was!

"Offy! Yukus!" he gasped, holding up the bit of his finger. It looked like a limp pink slug. "Help!" The healing snakes whipped into action, one taking his finger in its tail and pressing it to the stump, the other squirting golden liquid onto the wound from its fangs. Demon began to see stars, silver and green and purple, floating in front of his eyes. Then everything went black.

He woke to find himself sprawled beside the sleeping griffin, with a snake tongue tickling each earlobe. "Whaa . . . ?" he murmured, as his eyes focused again. He looked at his hand. It was a bit smeary with blood, but the finger was back as if it had never gone. "Oh, thank goodness," he said. "I don't know what I'd do without you two."

"A pleasure asss alwaysss, young massster," the snakes hissed.

Demon scrambled up and went to the hospital shed to wash. Then he smeared all the griffin's feathered bits with the new ointment. By the time he'd done his chores and followed all of Chiron's instructions, including making a bonfire of the straw in the beast's old pen, his eyes were closing on their own. He fell into bed, needing desperately to sleep, but every time he dropped off, he jerked awake again, worrying that another of his feathered beasts might have caught the Purple Spotted Feather Plague.

CHAPTER 5

OWL EMERGENCY

Dawn came far too soon. As Eos drew back her pink curtains, Demon sprang out of bed, seizing the huge bottle of green liquid. He put on his mask and went around every pen, sprinkling all the beasts and every inch of the Stables as he mucked out. The Caucasian Eagle was not at all pleased with being sprinkled, nor with being sent away to spend time with Prometheus.

"I have to peck his disgusting liver out every day—I don't need to socialize with the guy," it grumbled, giving Demon a sharp peck. "He keeps asking me to go and talk to Zeus's eagle for him, too. As if I'm some kind of best friends with that scary old bird." But it flapped off eventually, still grumbling, and promising not to come back till Demon sent word.

The winged horses were not enjoying the green liquid, either.

"It smells like rotten grass," they whinnied, rearing and bucking and battering him with their wings until Demon had to duck and dodge for fear of being trampled. He sniffed at it. It did stink a bit underneath—but it also smelled like nice things like eucalyptus, ginger, hyssop, lavender, and thyme.

"Do you really want all your feathers to fall out, and your skin to break out in purple popping spots?" he asked Keith, the boss winged horse, after the herd had calmed down a bit. Keith rubbed his tiny gold horns against Demon's shoulder.

"Nohohoho," he neighed, just as Demon heard a very strange noise outside the Stables.

Hic-a-hoot hic-a-hoot hic-a-hoot, it went.

He put down his bottle and went to investigate. As he saw the tall figure in silver armor approaching, his heart started to thump so hard that he could almost feel it trying to burst out of his ribs. Athena, goddess of wisdom, had come to visit, and in his experience, a visit from one of the Olympian gods or goddesses was never good news. Normally it led to threats of leg-twisting or seabed-scrubbing or plain old burnt-to-a-little-pile-of-charcoal-ing.

"Oh, do get up, Pandemonius," she said as he dropped to his knees in the dust. "There's no time for that. My poor Sophie here has got a terrible case of the upside-down hiccups. She just can't seem to stop." Athena made a face. "She keeps cuddling

up and giving me horrible, smelly owl kisses too."
As Athena spoke, the large owl on her rather
stained shoulder snuggled in under the goddess's
silver helmet and nibbled on her ear lovingly,
continuing to *hic-a-hoot*.
Suddenly, there
was a particularly
loud hiccup,
and out of
her beak shot a stream of
mangled mouse bones and
other more unmentionable things. Demon dodged
one particularly juicy something that splatted on
the ground at his feet with a wet squelch. *Oh no!*
he thought. *Just what I don't need—another sick
feathered creature!* What should he do? He had to
warn Athena about the plague, even if it made her
angry.

He cleared his throat, with a high squeaking

sound like a mouse whose tail has just been stepped on. "P-please don't bring her any closer, Your Wondrous Wiseness," he said, holding up a hand. "I don't want her to catch the Purple Spotted Feather Plague as well as the hiccups."

Athena stepped back hurriedly. "Explain, stable boy," she said, in the kind of voice that would have frozen any nearby volcanoes. "Fast." She pointed her silver spear at him menacingly, its sharp tip leveled right at his thumping heart.

So Demon explained, almost tripping over his words in an effort not to be stabbed.

"Very well, then," said Athena when he'd finished. "I shall leave Sophie roosting in one of my olive trees by the Iris Express. She'll be safe there, and then you can take her down to Chiron with the winged horses." She stroked the owl's soft feathers, looking worried, then frowned at Demon, her gray eyes flashing silver sparks. "You'd better have her cured by this afternoon, or I shall turn you into a nice fat black olive and crush you into oil," she said, turning to leave. "I've got to go and sort out an argument between Eos and Tithonus now, but I'll be down to collect her soon. Don't mess this up, Pandemonius. I've got a meeting with Zeus later, and he won't appreciate it if that big eagle of his catches whatever Sophie's got. Or the Purple Spotted Feather Plague, for that matter."

As the goddess left, Demon let out a sigh of relief so huge that it almost blew down the door of the Stables. Athena's silver spear had come so close to his heart, he'd almost felt it. But he couldn't think about that—or about being turned into an olive—because he had too much else to do.

"The griffin," he muttered. "Must see to the griffin." He trotted over to the isolation pen and put a cautious nose between the bars. The beast was still lying exactly where Demon had left it the night before, on its back. Loud, scratchy snores were coming from its beak, and its eyes were firmly closed.

"Griffin?" Demon said cautiously. "Griffin? Are you awake?" But there was no reply. The new pipe twiddle he'd learned from his dad was still working. He let himself into the pen and inspected the purple spots. They had definitely receded, though there were still a few left. Demon bent closer. Was that a new feather he saw? Yes! A row of new, tiny feathers had appeared right on top of the griffin's head. The ointment must be taking effect! He reached for the now half-empty pot and started to smear on another layer. There was no harm in putting on a little extra, just in case. Unfortunately, one of the bigger spots on the griffin's neck burst with a loud *POP!* just as he touched it. Horrid yellow slime leaked onto his hand and all over his tunic.

"YUCK!" he said, jumping back and grabbing a handful of straw to wipe it off. "I can see I'm going to be washing a LOT if this keeps happening."

Demon knew that when he eventually woke up the griffin, it'd be crankier than a cross manticore and hungrier than at least fifty packs of starving hellhounds. He'd need to find more than ambrosia cake if the beast wasn't to chomp on all his other fingers and toes—and probably the rest of him, as well.

He scratched his head absentmindedly, then shut the pen and went to scrub the yuck off and change. Maybe one of the kitchen fauns would help. But he'd have to find something to bribe it with. What did fauns like? Shells? He had some of those from his time down in Poseidon's watery kingdom. Or maybe he'd have to give up his spider-silk blanket . . .

Demon thought about this new problem all the

way to the kitchens, but he still hadn't come up with a suitable bribe by the time he got there. As usual, there was a riot of heat and good smells. His mouth watered as the scent of his favorite honey cakes reached his nose. Surely he could beg for just one?

A large hand fell on his shoulder, and he leaped into the air, letting out a squeal of fright.

"What are you doing sneaking around my kitchen, Pandemonius?" asked a voice like cream and honey on hot rocks. Oh no! He'd been caught by Hestia, goddess of cooking. She gave him a little shake. "Don't bother trying to lie to me, young stable boy, because I'll know." She took him by the ear and turned him around to face her.

"It's the griffin," Demon began. The story poured out of him for the second time that day. "And . . . and it says it needs a special diet of minced lamb with blood gravy and a sprinkle of scarab beetles," Demon finished.

Hestia frowned, tapping the silver ladle she held against her hip. "And what will you give me if I make the beast what it asks for?" she said. If thinking of something for a faun had been hard, thinking of something for a goddess was practically impossible. Demon didn't even try.

"What do you need, Your Goddessness?" he asked, trembling a little. "I'll give you anything."

She smiled. It was a smile with teeth in it. "Don't make rash promises to goddesses, Pandemonius. They can lead you into all sorts of trouble. Just tell my brother the centaur that I need a bunch of five-leaf panax and a pot of bee gold from his stores. Bring it with you when you return to Olympus. When I have it in my hands, I will make your beast its food—though I do draw the line at sprinkled scarabs." She ruffled his hair. "I have a soft spot for you, young stable boy. Heaven knows why!"

Demon looked up at her. "Th-thank you, Your

Amazingness," he stammered. He had no idea what
five-leaf panax or bee gold were, but he could find
out.

"Well, that's settled, then," said Hestia, towing
him into the kitchen behind her like a small
bobbing toy behind a very large boat. "Now, come
and taste my new batch of honey cakes."

CHAPTER 6

ATHENA'S TERRIBLE TASK

By the time Demon had licked the last of the honey cake from around his mouth, it was time to load the winged horses and Sophie the owl onto the Iris Express. The winged horses were very overexcited about their vacation and kept leaping into the air and doing little loop-de-loop somersaults. When Sophie saw him coming, she flapped out of her olive tree and onto his shoulder, wrapping one wing around his head and nibbling his ear lovingly— between hiccups. Demon peered around at her.

"Have you stopped spewing out mouse bones and stuff?" he asked. "Because this is my last clean tunic." Sophie just let out a mournful *hic-a-hoot* and snuggled in closer.

The Iris Express arrived in a flash of rainbow light, and soon Demon was busy trying to herd all the winged horses aboard.

"Go!" he shouted as the last hoof and tail crowded in. Demon tried not to look down. He was very near the edge, and there wasn't much room. Suddenly a familiar stench hit his nostrils.

"Oh no!" he said as he looked down. Tiny golden balls of horse poo were rolling around on the floor at his feet. "Who was that?" he asked sternly. The sturdy palomino mare called Sky Pearl hung her head.

"Meheeheehee," she neighed.

"Well, try not to, the rest of you," Demon said. "Iris won't like it."

"Indeed I will not," said Iris. Transparent rainbow arms picked up Sky Pearl under her wings and dangled her outside the rainbow. "If you do it again, I'll drop all of you into the sea. See how you like THAT!"

After that, the journey was not the smooth, swift ride Demon was used to. Iris bumped and jolted her passengers all the way down to Chiron's cave and spilled them out onto the ground. She left in a huff, snarling.

"Go and graze, all of you," Demon said. "And don't let them fly off, Keith."

"I wohohohon't," Keith whinnied, putting his head down and tearing at the long green grass.

"Now," said Demon. "Let's see if we can find some owl medicine." But just as he spoke, Sophie fell off his shoulder, flapping madly. She lay on the ground, eyes spinning like kaleidoscopes. An enormous *hic-a-hoot* erupted from her beak, and with it, a transparent pink heart-shaped bubble, followed by lots of smaller ones. Demon picked her up and stood her upright.

"What in the name of Athena's eyebrows is wrong with that owl?" asked a soft voice. Demon spun around. Standing astride two jagged rocks on the mountainside above was a tall nymph, dressed in floaty grays and greens and browns that made her look like a part of the stones themselves. She jumped down to join Peleus, who came out of the cave, a great big smile on his face. He was brandishing a shiny silver sword, which flashed shards of sunlight into Demon's eyes, making him blink.

"Look, Demon!" he said. "The wolves found it for me! Thank you ever so much. I owe you a massive favor. Whatever you want, really, just ask!" He put an arm around the tall nymph. "This is my mom, Endeis, by the way. She's the oread of this mountain."

"You have my gratitude, too, Pandemonius," said Endeis. "You did a very brave thing, saving my son from those centaurs. But we can talk about that later. Right now your owl definitely has a problem that needs fixing."

Demon wasn't going to disagree. Sophie was now *hic-a-hoot*-ing so fast that the pink heart bubbles had formed a thick cloud around both of them. Quickly, he picked her up and ran into the cave. Surely there must be something about curing hiccups in one of Chiron's books. Although he'd never heard of anyone hiccuping out pink hearts.

"What have you eaten, Sophie?" he asked. But the owl couldn't answer. She was too busy hiccuping and trying to give Demon more owl kisses.

"Stop it," Demon said, fending her off. "If you can't speak, then you'll have to flap. Once for yes, twice for no, all right?" Sophie flapped once.

"Did you eat anything you wouldn't normally eat?"

Flap.

"Did someone give it to you?"

Flap. Flap.

Endeis interrupted.

"Did you steal it from one of the gods?" she asked. Demon didn't know that nymphs could speak owl. He thought it was only him.

Sophie's eyes started to spin the other way, and she hiccuped out a very small heart.

Flap.

All at once Demon remembered something Hephaestus had said. "Have you been anywhere near Eros?" he asked. "Did you swallow something with a love potion in it?"

Flap.

"Right," said Demon. "That's it! I've seen a love-potion antidote somewhere. Chiron had to make one up the other day for some poor girl who'd fallen in love with a tree."

Peleus laughed. "A tree? Are you serious?"

"Deadly serious," said Demon, searching along the shelves. "She made little garlands for its branches and everything. Said she wanted to marry it. That was one of Eros's potions, too. He said it was a joke." He closed his lips tightly in case he'd said something he shouldn't. Even if Eros was a god, he shouldn't play tricks like that. It wasn't very kind.

"Is this it?" asked Endeis, holding up a clear bottle of bright-blue potion.

"Yes!" said Demon. "Quick! Pass it here!"

It took five drops of potion for Sophie's eyes to go back to normal and for the pink hearts to stop. She was just explaining how she'd eaten some tasty sugar mice she'd found in Eros's room, when Athena arrived. Her eyes were wild, and her silver helmet was all askew. Sophie flew straight to her shoulder, but the goddess was so distracted that she didn't even seem to notice that her owl was cured.

"Where's Chiron?" she asked Demon. "I need him. Immediately."

"I'm afraid he doesn't seem to be here, Your Wiseness."

"Well, go and fetch him at once. Run, boy! Run! It's an emergency!" Demon looked around at Peleus and Endeis frantically. He had no idea where his teacher had gone, nor any clue where to look.

"It's no use for Pandemonius to run anywhere," Endeis said. "My father's gone off to tend Asclepius's baby. There were complications with the birth. He left a message with me. He won't be back for at least a week, and he's not to be disturbed."

Athena stamped her foot. A small crack appeared in the mountainside, and the ground shook.

Endeis took a step forward. "Mind my mountain," she said crossly. "You'll break it."

Athena turned on her and roared. Silver sparks shot out of her eyes, skittering across the ground, where they fell, making the grass curl and shrivel. "Wretched nymph," she shouted. "Your stupid father is NEVER where he's supposed to be. Who's going to cure that wretched phoenix now?"

Her sparking eyes fell on Demon. "You! Pandemonius! You'll have to do it."

"M-m-me?"

"Yes, you! The beastly bird has gone blind and lost its voice just when it needs to build its nest. I just got a fire message from Antaeus, who I've told to guard the beast." She stamped her foot again, and a jagged trench opened up at Demon's feet. "Why now?" the goddess yelled, flinging her helmet on the ground and stamping on it. "Just when Zeus has commanded me to help some wretched hero son of his kill a Gorgon." Her eyes fell on Demon again and she flapped a hand at him, emitting a shower of stinging silver darts. "Go!" she said. "Why are you still here?"

"I-I don't know where to go, Your Knowledgeableness," he said, feeling his stomach drop into his toes as he dodged the darts rather unsuccessfully. They pierced his skin, burning like the stings of a thousand wasps. Was this it? Was he finally going to be turned into cinders?

Athena tutted impatiently. "Do you know nothing? The phoenix lives in a cave at the top of the Mountains of Burning Sand, right in the middle of a desert. The Iris Express knows where." She glared at him. "If it isn't able to sing its Song of Renewal at the right moment, then the fire devils it guards will escape and steal all its power. Do you know what that means, stable boy?"

Demon shook his head, picking darts out of his ears.

"You like birds and beasts, don't you, Pandemonius?"

He nodded as Athena bent toward him.

"If the fire devils are let loose on the world, they will burn up the nearby forest where millions of the most wonderful creatures on earth live. Every death will give the fire devils more power—and then they will turn on US!"

She hissed like a striking snake and lifted him

up by the front of his tunic till their noses were nearly touching. "If you don't cure that bird so that it can sing its Song of Renewal, you will be responsible for the deaths of all those beasts—and maybe even the safety of Olympus itself!" Her voice dropped to a low growl. "Don't fail me, Pandemonius. Or I will ask Father Zeus to take care of you personally. And I don't mean with ambrosia and honey cakes."

With that, the goddess shot up into the air, faster than a streak of silver lightning, and disappeared, leaving a wavering hoot of farewell from Sophie lingering in the air.

"Oh no!" Demon whispered, sinking to his knees as he picked slivers of silver out of his shoulder and chest. It was his most impossible task yet.

CHAPTER 7
HORRIBLE HERACLES STRIKES AGAIN

"No time for that," said Endeis, hauling him to his feet. "Pack what you need while I call the Iris Express for you."

As he rushed into the cave, Demon's thoughts whirled madly, like snowflakes in a blizzard. What would he need? "Eyebright and chamomile for blindness, slippery elm and marshmallow for sore throats, aloe for burns," he panted, throwing bandages, bowls, cloths, and everything else he could think of into one of Chiron's herb-gathering sacks.

"And this," said Peleus, holding out Chiron's own personal Book of Cures. The one that was chained to the wall.

"I can't take that," said Demon. "Chiron said it must never leave the cave."

"Well, he's not here. And it's an emergency," said Peleus, unhooking it. So Demon stowed it in the sack, along with his opticles. Was that everything he needed?

"Oh no!" he groaned. "My pyro-protection suit! It's back on Olympus. I'll have to go and get it. I'll get burnt up by those fire devils otherwise." He rushed outside, only to see the Iris Express disappearing into the sky.

"Nooo! Iris," he called, "come back! Please! I need you!" But there was no answer, only the splatting sound of a pile of liquid winged-horse poo falling at his feet.

"She's gone on strike," Endeis said. "Said she's

never carrying you again till you apologize at least three times on your bended knees and scrub her inside out twenty times till she's shiny again. One of those winged horses had another poo accident before they landed, apparently. Rather a runny one, as you can see."

Demon's whole body felt hollow, as if his skin was going to collapse. Prickles of cold ran all over him. There was no chance of getting his pyro-protection suit—or anything else from Olympus—now. "What am I going to do?" he whispered. "However am I going to get to the Mountains of Burning Sand? The phoenix won't be able to sing, the fire devils will escape, and all those wonderful creatures will be burnt up." He gulped. "And what if they burn up the gods and goddesses, too? What will happen to us all?" He didn't even want to think about that—or about Zeus himself coming after him. He wouldn't even be a pile of charcoal if that happened. He'd be nothing at all.

"Mountains of Burning Sahahahand?" neighed Keith, flying over the jagged trench that now cut off access to the cave. "Thahahat's near our earthly home."

Demon turned to him eagerly. "Do you know the way there, Keith? Could you take me?"

The little boss winged horse swished his black tail. "Maybe," he whinnied. "If I get a LOT of itchy-scratches."

"I'll give you as many itchy-scratches as you want," Demon said, flinging his arms around Keith's neck. "How far is it? Can we get there quickly?"

Keith shook his head, his mane flying into Demon's eyes. "It's a long wayheyhey," he snorted. Demon groaned. How could he leave his beasts again—and what about the griffin? Would it really stay asleep until Demon got back? As usual, he didn't have a choice. Curing the phoenix was more important than anything—but he was still worried.

"Who's going to look after the Stables?" he said. "If they begin to smell of poo again, I'll have the goddesses after me as well as Zeus."

"I'll do it," said Endeis. "I can visit my nymph and dryad friends at the same time. I haven't seen Althea for ages. I've been too busy being queen and taking care of things back at the palace on Aegina." She frowned. "It'll do them all good to be without me for a while."

"I've decided I'm coming with you to the Mountains of Burning Sand," said Peleus. "You might need a friend to guard your back. Those fire devils sound dangerous. Anyway, it'll be an adventure." He grinned, winking at Demon with one bright green eye.

Demon looked at Peleus doubtfully. He was quite tall. "I'm not sure you'll fit on a winged horse," he said.

"I'll carry him," said Sky Pearl, trotting forward. "I'm strong."

Quickly Demon and Peleus loaded up the medicine sack and another bag full of food and waterskins. They also found some ropes, which they tied around themselves and the little horses.

"Just in case we fall asleep or need to haul each other up the mountain," Peleus said as he slung his sword across his back and climbed onto Sky Pearl. He did look a bit funny, with his long legs dangling nearly to the ground, but Demon didn't feel much like laughing. He had a blind, voiceless phoenix to cure—and he hadn't a clue how to do it.

They flew and flew until the bones in their bottoms ached from sitting, over land, over sea, and then over land again. As Helios and his chariot rolled through the sky above them, Demon waved to his friend Abraxas and the other celestial horses.

Soon it was night. The stars shone
cold and distant, like diamonds on deep
blue velvet. Demon tried to count them to pass
the time, but all too quickly he felt his eyelids
drooping.

"Ooh," he said, wriggling to get comfortable.
"However am I going to keep awake?" He clutched
at Keith's mane, winding it around and around his
wrists.

"Ouchy!" Keith whinnied. "Don't hold on so
hard! And stop wiggling around!"

"Lucky we tied ourselves on!" Peleus called over. "I'm sleepy, too."

"Tell us about the Mountains of Burning Sand, Keith," said Demon. "And about whatsisname? Antaeus? Maybe that'll keep us from falling asleep."

"Antaeus is a giant," Keith whinnied. "Big as a mountain. We don't go near him. He has a nasty club. He likes to fight."

Naturally, Athena hadn't bothered to say anything about a giant, Demon thought. That was so typical of the gods—they never thought you needed to know things like that.

"That sounds scary," he said, shivering. He'd never met a giant—and he wasn't sure he wanted to.

"Is scary," neighed Sky Pearl. "Smells bad, too. Like rotten blood."

"I knew you'd need me, Demon," said Peleus cheerfully. "I'll fight him. I've fought LOTS of people with my magic sword. I never, ever lose.

Well, almost never," he added.

"But he's a GIANT!" Demon said.

"So?" said Peleus boastfully. "My sword is sharp, and I fear nothing and nobody." Demon thought about how nervous Peleus had looked around the wolves, but wisely chose not to mention it.

As they flew into the dawn of another day, Demon began to smell a spicy green scent wafting up from below. As Eos's pink light started to fill the east, he saw a vast expanse of forest below them.

"Is that the place Athena talked about?" he asked. "The one with all the amazing creatures in it?"

"Yes," Keith neighed. "Look! There's a herd of tall-necks! See? In the glade."

Demon peered down. The most extraordinary animals he'd ever seen were grazing the treetops. They had long necks that allowed them to reach the topmost branches, and tiny snail-shaped horns.

They were spotty and dappled, like shade, and their backs sloped downward, so their legs were shorter at the back than at the front. Demon longed to ask Keith to land. He desperately wanted to talk to them, but he knew he mustn't. Instead he must save the phoenix so that these marvelous creatures weren't all burnt up.

"How far to go?" he asked, wishing that Keith's poor little wings could flap even faster.

"Still far," Keith whinnied. "But you can see the mountains now—and the desert." In the distance, golden peaks caught the first rays from Helios, turning them to a blaze of red flame. As they flew through the day, the mountains grew bigger and bigger until they made everything around them seem dwarflike.

As dusk fell, Demon could see a tiny figure leaping and running across the sand, toward the forest. "I wonder who that is," he said.

"Going down!" Sky Pearl and Keith called as they dipped their wings, gliding toward a flat piece of land outside a cave in the rocks. It was covered in a carpet of tiny golden flowers that gave off a scent like honey. A stone well with a bucket beside it stood nearby.

"Sand flowers!" Sky Pearl whinnied, burying her nose in the fragrant blossoms. "Yummy-scrum!"

Keith skidded to a halt beside her, his wings drooping. "Itchy-scratch?" he asked hopefully as Demon untied himself and clambered off, legs as limp as jellied sand snakes. Demon gave the boss horse's ears a good scratching as Keith, too, buried his nose in the flowers and started munching.

"Hey!" Peleus shouted from the direction of the cave. "Come over here! I don't think I'm going to have to fight the giant, after all—someone's already done it!"

Demon grabbed his healing sack and stumbled

over to the dark entrance. Sticking out of it were two thick, hairy legs, with rusty iron shin guards buckled around them. As Demon clambered past, he saw Peleus squatting beside the giant's enormous head. Antaeus was almost as broad as he was tall, with more iron armor strapped to his arms and chest. The vast, sausage-like fingers on his left hand lay limp around a huge spiked club. Over his shoulders hung a hooded cloak of shimmering feathers that shone and shifted like fire and lit up the rest of the cave. Demon's breath caught in his throat as the blank, black eyes of a thousand skulls looked down at him. At least they weren't alive like the ones he'd met in Hades's Underworld kingdom.

"Is he breathing?" he asked anxiously.

There was no time to be scared.

"I think so," said Peleus.

"Someone's given him a big whack on the head, though. Look!" Lifting the giant's short, red hair, he pointed to a big purple lump on his already knobby forehead.

Demon shook the gigantic shoulder. "Antaeus! Antaeus! Wake up!"

CHAPTER 8

FIREFALL

"NYAARRGHH!" shouted the giant in a great rumbling voice. He sat up so suddenly that he knocked Peleus head over heels. "Wassermatter?" The giant looked around wildly. "Where is he? Where's that Heracles? Let me at him!" Then, quite suddenly, his eyes rolled back in his head and he slumped again, quite unconscious. Demon jumped up, fists clenched. An angry ball of rage flared up inside his belly as he glared around the cave. Horrible Heracles? Was he still here? He eyed Antaeus's club. Would he be strong enough to lift it? He owed Heracles a few good whacks for being so nasty to the poor beasts in the Stables. And now he'd knocked out the very person Demon needed most! Then Demon remembered the tiny running figure he'd seen as they'd flown over the desert.

"Drat!" he said. It was no use. The beast-bashing hero would be far away by now. "I'll get you one day, horrible Heracles," he muttered.

Sighing, he shook the giant's armor-clad shoulder again, but there was no response.

"Burning feathers," he muttered. "That's what I need." Quickly, he pulled a handful of the shining plumes out of Antaeus's cloak and lit them at the tiny covered fire that burned in the cave. Immediately, there was a smell of singed cinnamon and spice mixed with something that caught at the back of his throat and made him cough. He blew out the flame and waved the smoking feathers under Antaeus's nose.

"Gaarrgh!" the giant exclaimed, sitting up again. "What is that disgusting smell?" He fanned one of his enormous hands in front of his face. Then he howled, clutching at chest. "Ow! My ribs!"

"Are you properly awake now?" Demon asked. "Athena got your message. She's sent me to heal the phoenix. Can you take us to it?"

"Phoenix?" Antaeus asked, rubbing his head in a confused way. "What phoenix? I don't know what you're talking about." He looked around. "Where's that pesky Heracles gone? I need his skull for my collection!" He blinked sleepily. "And who are you two, my little shrimps? You're not big enough or ugly enough to be heroes."

"I'm Peleus, he's Demon, and never mind about Heracles," Peleus said impatiently. "The phoenix is what's important now. You know . . . the one you're supposed to be guarding? The one that's gone blind and has no voice?"

"Still not with you," said the giant, picking his nose and inspecting the slimy green result before popping it into his mouth.

"It's that bump. He's had all the sense knocked out of him by Heracles," said Demon, pulling ointment and bandages out of his sack. "Quick! Go and get him some water from the well. That might help his memory."

"You get it," said Peleus sulkily. "I'm a prince, not your servant." Then he saw the fierce look in Demon's eyes. "Oh, all right," he grumbled. "I'll give the winged horses some first, though. They must be thirsty."

Demon immediately felt bad. He should have thought of that. Quickly, he smeared bruise-flower ointment on the bump and rolled bandages around Antaeus's ribs under the armor. It was really hard because the giant groaned and wriggled around. He was being much more difficult than any of Demon's beast patients.

"Don't be such a baby," Demon said, just as Peleus came back, puffing and slopping water everywhere.

"This stuff tastes amazing," the prince said. "Like liquid sunlight." It was true. The water in the bucket glowed slightly.

"Maybe it'll help," said Demon hopefully. He filled a clay cup and put it to the giant's lips. Antaeus slurped it down, dribbling it disgustingly down his front.

"More," he said. After sixteen more cups, he burped loudly. "Marvelous stuff," he said. "My magic well always does the trick." Then he clapped a hand to his forehead, where the bump had already disappeared. "The phoenix! I remember now." He looked around. "Where's old Chiron, then? The poor creature is in great need. It's gotten much worse since I sent Athena that message."

"Athena sent me instead," said Demon.

Antaeus looked down at him doubtfully. "A bit small for a healer, aren't you?"

"Never mind my size," said Demon crossly. "Do you want the phoenix fixed or not? Athena said it was pretty urgent."

"And so it is, shrimp boy," said Antaeus. "Come on, then. Up on my shoulders, the both of you. I'll have you there faster than Apollo can fire an arrow."

"Let's take some of that magic water with us," said Peleus. "It might come in handy."

"Good thinking," said Antaeus. Demon nodded a bit sourly. That was another thing he should have thought of first.

Once the waterskins were full, and Demon had made sure that the winged horses were happy, the giant grabbed Demon in one hand and Peleus in the other, tossing them and the bags into the air and onto his shoulders as if they were straws. The armor wasn't very comfortable to sit on, though the feather cloak gave them a bit of padding. They had to hang on to the giant's ears to avoid being joggled off as Antaeus ran up the side of the mountain faster than a shooting star.

As they neared the top, he skidded to a halt outside a rather grand cave. It had crumbling pillars on either side of it that were carved with very ancient-looking pictures of flames, strange-looking birds, eggs, and suns. That wasn't what caught Demon's eye, though. Covering the whole entrance was a golden cascade, not of water, but of fire that lit up the night like a torch.

"Through there!" Antaeus said as Demon and Peleus slid down to the ground, landing with two loud bumps that raised clouds of sparkling dust.

Demon gaped at him. "How do we get through *that*?" he asked, pointing at the firefall. "We'll get all burned up! Is there no other way through?"

Antaeus shook his head.

"How do you get in, then?" Peleus asked.

"With this, of course," said Antaeus, pointing to his cloak. "It's made of phoenix feathers. They're flameproof." He fumbled in a pocket, pulling out a mask that was also made of feathers. "And I put this on, too."

"You'll have to take us in underneath your cloak, then," said Demon. "There's no time to lose."

"There's not a lot of room," said Peleus. "We'll have to go one at a time."

"Well, I'm going first," said Demon, grabbing the medicine sack. "I'm not leaving that poor bird a moment longer than I have to."

"Brave little shrimp," said Antaeus, throwing the cloak wide. "Crawl under!"

"Don't call me that," Demon said as Antaeus settled him in the crook of one arm and pulled the cloak shut tight again. But Antaeus just laughed—a great earthquake rumble that shook Demon right down to his toes.

Demon had never felt heat like it, not even when Hera had nearly sizzled him to a frazzle. There was a blinding flash as his feet began to frizzle, and then they were through. Antaeus let Demon down, then went back for Peleus. Demon checked to see that his toes were all still there, then looked around wonderingly. The cave walls were made of a buttery-smooth white stone that had soft lights flickering within it, changing from rose to pale green to the exact soft blue of an early-morning sky. The walls went up and up. At the top, crystal stalactites hung down like rainbow daggers, reflecting the lights from below. The floor was not white, though, but shining black, and right in the middle of it sat a gigantic ruby, its center glowing and pulsing weakly like a heart in trouble. Around it was a messy pile of sweetly scented branches, some long, some short, mixed all higgledy-piggledy with slivers of bark, dried flowers, bright fruits, and bunches of various berries. Slumped on top of the ruby was a huge bird. Demon could tell immediately that it was in trouble. Its head lolled over the edge, and its long, flowing tail feathers were dull and lifeless. Then it coughed, a horrible, weak tearing sound, which Demon immediately knew was not a good sign.

"Oh, you poor thing," he said, running to it. But the ruby towered over him, and jump as he might,

he couldn't get a grip to clamber up its slippery sides.

"Hey!" said Peleus behind him. "Look at the fire devils!" He pointed to the back of the cave. In his hurry to reach the phoenix, Demon hadn't even noticed the transparent crystal wall half hidden by the bulk of the ruby. Suddenly he felt as if a large fist had slammed into his chest. Behind the crystal were skinny red creatures, capering and shrieking gleefully. They had unnaturally long arms and legs, and sharp-clawed hands and feet. Their heads were huge, and their eyes were pits of dark flame. It was the mouths that were the worst, though. They gaped hungrily, showing rows of needle-sharp teeth, and each mouth blew out a jet of blue-white flame that skittered over the surface of their prison.

"Oh no," said Demon, his voice trembling. At the top of the crystal wall there was a very small crack.

CHAPTER 9

NEST OF ANTS

"I'll fight them off if they escape," Peleus said, drawing his magic sword with a flash of silver lightning. "You help that bird." He struck a pose and menaced the fire devils, waving his blade around threateningly. But the fire devils took no notice. They just shrieked and capered even more. Peleus beat his chest with his free hand, uttering whooping war cries. "Defy me at your peril, foul creatures," he yelled. "You shall not pass Peleus."

"Poor little phoenix," Antaeus crooned, lowering

the creature tenderly and laying it on the ground at Demon's feet. Peleus continued to shout defiantly behind them. Demon knelt down beside the phoenix, stroking it gently. It was limp all over, with its crest and tail drooping sadly, and its eyelids were stuck together with a grayish-white film of gunk. When Demon gently opened its long beak to take a look inside, he found that its throat was nearly clogged shut by a gloopy orange substance. It smelled hot and throat-chokingly bitter—like badly burnt caramel. The phoenix's thin, pointed tongue was covered in red pustules. Demon had never seen anything like it, and if he had wished for his magical medicine box to cure the griffin, he wished for it a million times more now. What he did have, though, was Chiron's very own precious Book of Cures. Quickly he got it out and put on his opticles.

"*E* for *Eyes*," he said, flicking through the pages

frantically. Unfortunately the writing inside made no sense. He could read the letters, but it seemed to be set out in some sort of secret code.

Mix Euph. x 1 grain plus Loc. Pers. x 5 meas.

"What in Aphrodite's underpants does that mean?" he wailed. It was worse than the stupid language the medicine box used. He'd have to do his best to find a cure for the phoenix on his own. Scrabbling in the sack again, he pulled out everything he'd brought with him, thinking hard about what he'd learned from Chiron.

"This, this, and . . . yes . . . this," he said, dumping a few pinches of all the things he knew might work in a wooden bowl and pounding them together. Then he added a good splash of the magic water. Taking a clean cloth, he gently bathed away the gray gunk till it was all gone. The phoenix blinked. There was still a gray film over its eyes, so Demon dripped in some more of the mixture.

Slowly the gray cleared away. He could see the phoenix's beautiful gold irises and silver pupils, all surrounded by a circle of bright ruby red.

"You seem to be a healer, after all, little shrimp," said Antaeus. "Though I'm sure most of it was my well water."

"I don't care what did it, as long as it works," Demon said, before putting together a different bunch of herbs, making up a soothing milky potion with more of the magic water. Before he could get the bird to swallow, though, he had to put two fingers in its throat and clear out the orange gloop. It was horrible and messy, and it burnt his skin, but finally it was done. He tipped in the throat mix in small drops. The red pustules disappeared almost immediately, and the phoenix began to look a bit perkier. A little color even started to return to its tail feathers, and then, all of a sudden, it hopped upright.

"Can you sing?" Demon asked anxiously.

It cocked its head to one side and opened its beak. A harsh croaking sound erupted from its throat.

"That sounds more like a dying crow than a song," said Demon, trying not to despair. "Let's try some more medicine." But the bird shook its head, turning away its beak. It pointed one sharp claw and started to scratch something on the floor of the cave. Unfortunately, the claw made no impression on the shiny black stone.

"Are you trying to show me what will help?" Demon asked. The phoenix nodded.

"Here," said Demon, holding out a pot of the white clay he used for making ointment. "Try this." The phoenix dipped its claw in the thick liquid and started to scratch again. Immediately, something began to take shape. Demon frowned. It couldn't be. But it was. The phoenix had drawn a gigantic ant.

"Is that an ant?" he asked. "How can an ant help?" He turned to Antaeus, whose brown skin had now gone a kind of ashy gray. "Do you know anything about ants?"

"Y-yes," said the giant, not meeting Demon's eyes.

"Well?" Demon said impatiently.

"There's a nest of giant golden fire ants right on top of this mountain. I've never met them, though. They keep themselves to themselves." Antaeus jerked the words out quickly, as if he didn't want to say them. It almost sounded like he was afraid.

Demon turned back to the phoenix. "Do you need one of the ants to come to you?" he asked. It shook its head and dipped its claw in the pot of clay again. This time it drew a circle with a second jagged circle within it, then tapped the circle several times with its claw. It looked like a wonky dewdrop. Demon scrubbed his hands through his hair, making it stand up on end. What could it mean? Just as he was about to ask Peleus what he thought, a sharp *crack* sounded behind him. Demon spun around as the fire devils' shrieking reached a new pitch.

"Oops!" said Peleus. There was now a long, blade-shaped gash in the crystal, and a new crack had started. The fire devils were scraping at it eagerly with their claws and blowing out more jets of white-hot flame.

"You idiot!" Antaeus and Demon roared at the same time. The phoenix let out another harsh croak and started jumping up and down with rage, lunging at Peleus with its beak.

"I'm sorry, I'm sorry," he said, holding up a hand. "My bad. I slipped."

"Well, stop waving that thing around and come and help us figure out this picture," said Demon. "You're making things worse, not better."

As soon as he saw the picture of the ant, and the circle beside it, Peleus smiled. "Easy," he said. "That's a ball of ant nectar. Is that what you need, Phoenix?" The phoenix immediately stopped trying to skewer him with its beak and nodded enthusiastically. "Can you take us to the colony, Antaeus? I think I can help you get some."

"Is this more of your stupid boasting?" Demon asked, still angry with the prince.

Peleus shook his head. "No. I promise." But however much Demon pestered him, he would say no more.

Demon didn't want to leave the phoenix, but it shooed him out of the cave with its wings, croaking like a mad frog.

Once they were safely through the firefall again, Antaeus was very reluctant to take them to the peak of the mountain.

"Do you actually want us all to be burnt up by the fire devils?" Demon shouted at him.

Antaeus hung his huge head. "No," he said. But as they got near the peak, which was sparkling golden pink in the early light, his run changed to a trot and then to a walk that got slower and slower.

Suddenly, up ahead, Demon spotted a mass of segmented bright red ants, feelers waving in the air. They were almost as big as the giant scorpion. They bobbed up and down, bowing to Helios's chariot as it drove over the eastern horizon, pulling the sun behind it.

Antaeus began to shake as he saw them. "Ugh!" he said, his whole body shuddering till his armor rattled. "Ugh! Ugh! Ugh! Too many legs! It's unnatural!" Antaeus dumped Demon and Peleus unceremoniously on the ground, fled to a nearby rock, and cowered behind it.

Demon looked back at him, his mouth open. Now he understood. Antaeus was afraid of insects. He was about to ask Peleus what he thought they should do next when he realized the prince had disappeared from beside him.

Peleus was up ahead, right in among the ants, whirling around in an odd kind of dance. He began to make a strange clicking sound. Then he drew his sword and started to wave it around again. The silver blade caught the sun's rays, making a net of fiery lines in the air. Demon couldn't believe what he was seeing.

"You idiot!" he screamed at Peleus for the second time that day. "You'll ruin everything!"

CHAPTER 10

THE QUEEN'S MEDICINE

Even as the words left Demon's mouth, the ants started to dance with Peleus, making the same strange clicking sounds back at him. Demon soon realized that they were talking to one another. Despite his gift for understanding animals, he could only understand a few of the words—and those didn't make much sense to him. Insect language was really hard. He'd only had the giant scorpion to practice on, and it didn't talk much. How did Peleus know ant language? How could he speak it?

There was no time to ask. Peleus stood on the backs of two ants, looking like a young god and clicking even louder. He gestured toward Demon with one hand. Before Demon knew what was happening, a monstrous ant warrior was running toward him on its spindly legs. Its pincer jaws seized him around the shoulders and dragged him to the huge mound of its nest.

"Help!" Demon cried out, trying to kick it. "Let me go! Help! Peleus! What's going on? Antaeus! Save me!" But Peleus had disappeared into the round nest entrance, and Antaeus was still hiding behind his rock. As the ant jaws dug into the tops of his shoulders like knives, Demon didn't dare say any more,

afraid they would nip his
dangling arms right off.
Where was Peleus
now? How could he
have betrayed

Demon like this? And why? Was this all some
mysterious plot to make him into ant food? A hot,
angry tear ran down Demon's cheek. He'd really
thought Peleus was a friend.

Deeper and deeper into the nest they ran,
Demon's poor toes dragging and bumping along the
floor. The network of strangely beautiful tunnels
twisted and turned, so that Demon was soon
lost and giddy. All he knew was that they were
going downward, and that the heat was getting
unbearable, as was the dry,
acid smell of insect.

Sweat dripped down his face, getting into his eyes, burning and stinging. The endless clicking of ant talk echoed through the nest.

"Please, Dad, please, great Pan, help me to understand," he whispered. Maybe if he knew what the ants were saying, he could talk to them. He could explain that this was all a big mistake and tell them that all he wanted was some ant medicine for the poor phoenix. So it could sing its song. Wouldn't they all get burnt up, too, if the fire devils escaped? Surely they'd care about that.

A breeze touched him, cool and green, smelling of forests and deep, still pools. *Touch my pipes!* said a low, moss-velvet voice inside Demon's head.

"Dad?" he gasped, trying to crane his head around. But Pan wasn't there. Cautiously, and with great difficulty, Demon managed to get his little finger inside his tunic, to where Pan's silver pipes were stowed. The effect was immediate. As soon as he touched them, he heard a loud, chittering chant.

"Hail to Peleus! Hail to the Prince of the Myrmidons!"

"What in the name of Aphrodite's nightie are Myrmidons?" Demon asked. His captor ran into a big open chamber crammed full of a seething swarm of insects, and dropped him, sprawling, between the front legs of a massive queen ant. She was *twice* the size of her subjects, and her segmented red body glittered with golden specks. Before he could get to his feet, Demon felt a hand at the back of his damp and sweaty tunic, pulling him up and dusting him off. It was Peleus.

"You!" Demon hissed, his face turning a scarlet so furious that he thought he might burst into flames. "What do you think you're doing?"

"Helping you get what you need," said Peleus cheerfully. "Now *shh!*" Then he bowed low to the gigantic ant before Demon could say that he didn't want to *shh* one little bit.

"Your Majesty," Peleus said, in the clicking ant tongue. "I bring you greetings from your human ant cousins, the Myrmidons, and from my father, their king. May your feelers ever prosper and your children number millions." Demon's mouth fell open. Peleus's father was the king of the human ants? He'd never mentioned that before. Well, that explained a few things!

"Greetings, Prince of Ants," said the queen. "And who is this small human you bring before me?" She bent forward, stroking her feelers over Demon's body till he had to bite his lip to keep from laughing. It felt very tickly. "Is he a gift? Is he my breakfast?" As soon as Demon heard her say that, the urge to laugh left him very quickly, replaced by a cold wash of fear. He clenched his fists to stop them from trembling.

"This is Pandemonius, son of the great Pan. He is my friend and companion on a quest set by wise Athena," said Peleus hurriedly. "We need your help to save the phoenix and stop the fire devils from escaping into the world."

"And how may I do that?" the queen asked. But before Peleus could answer, there was a great banging and shaking. As the floor trembled, Demon gasped. Had the fire devils escaped already? Was this the end? Were they all to be burnt up? He was sure he could feel the floor getting even hotter under his feet.

But then he heard a familiar voice shouting. Antaeus had found his courage at last and come to the rescue!

"Peleus! Demon! Where are you? Let me in!" yelled the giant, his gruff tones echoing through the nest, which shook from his repeated blows. With an enraged chittering and clicking, the ant warriors charged out of the queen's chamber and back toward the surface.

"Oh no!" said Peleus. "Stupid giant! They'll kill him! I'd better go and tell him we're all right, before he's stung to death." He sprinted after the horde of ants, leaving Demon alone with the queen and her attendants.

The queen tapped one pointy foot on the floor as Demon eyed her enormous pincerlike jaws. She could munch him up in an instant. "Well?" she asked. "What have you to say for yourself, small human?"

Demon took a deep breath, trying not to think of being eaten. "Well, Your Majesty," he said, stumbling a bit as he got his tongue around the difficult clicks. "The phoenix thought you might have some special medicine." He drew a round shape in the air with his hands. "In a ball. Nectar, Peleus called it." He looked up into the queen's

glittering eyes,
willing her to help.
"If the fire devils
escape, it will be
a disaster. This
mountain will
be the first to
get burnt up.
And if I can't
cure the phoenix's
voice so it can sing again, that's what
will happen, and there's very little
time left. The fire devil prison
already has cracks in it." His
voice broke. "It's . . . it's a real
emergency, Your Majestic
Antness."

The queen didn't waste any time. She turned to two of her attendants and clapped her front legs together. "Fetch me two globes of sweet acid nectar at once," she commanded. "Hurry!" She looked down at Demon. "If the Prince of Ants had not brought you, I should have considered you a juicy morning snack," she said. "You do know that, don't you?"

Demon nodded, just as the attendants scurried back, each carrying a round globe full of a milky liquid. Now he felt ashamed of doubting Peleus. He was indeed a true friend.

"Thank you for not eating me, Your Majesty," he said, tucking a globe carefully under each arm. They wobbled slightly, like jelly.

"Don't squash them," said the queen sharply. "Now go! I have no wish to be burnt up in my bed."

Demon ran as quickly as he dared. He didn't want the queen changing her mind.

CHAPTER 11

PHOENIX SONG

As Demon emerged from the heat of the ant mound, he took in great gulps of fresh air. Antaeus and Peleus were waiting outside, surrounded by ant warriors. Antaeus still looked nervous, glancing around him with wild eyes, but his armor had obviously fended off the worst of the stings. Suddenly, the mountain gave a shudder. This time it was not Antaeus.

"Quick," Demon said, his heart clenching with dread. "Down the mountain. We must get back to the phoenix."

Antaeus scooped up him and Peleus at once, being extra-careful of the fragile sweet-acid globes.

"Good-bye, my ant brothers!" called Peleus to the warriors.

"Farewell, Prince of Ants," they clicked back as the giant sprinted down the mountain so fast that the rocks became no more than a golden blur under his feet.

As they approached the phoenix's cave, the ground shuddered harder. Antaeus threw his feather cloak over both of them and ran through the firefall. There was no time to waste. Burns would mend, but not if the phoenix wasn't saved.

The floor of the cave was rippling like tiny black waves, and a thick smell of burning sulfur filled the air. A third and much larger crack had appeared in the crystal wall, and Demon was horrified to see that white-hot sparks were fizzing through it. The fire devils were screeching with triumph. They were nearly free. Demon jumped to the ground, almost falling on the unsteady floor in his panic to get to the phoenix.

"Steady," said Peleus as Demon handed him the second globe before cracking the first in half, like an egg. "Don't spill it!"

Demon didn't answer. He was too busy tipping the sweet-sour-smelling liquid down the phoenix's gaping beak. One half went in, then the other.

"C'mon," he whispered. "C'mon! Work!"

All at once, the phoenix started to shine, all the way from beak to tail. Light poured out of its feathers in shades of flame from brightest white to deepest red, so dazzling that Demon had to cover his eyes. Its long tail feathers fanned out with a crisp snap like jade-gold lightning. Backing away, Demon took shelter under Antaeus's cloak, where Peleus was already crouched.

Then, with a flap like a billowing sail, the

phoenix's wings opened. It soared high up to the ceiling of the cave before swooping down to seize branch after branch. Almost quicker than the eye could see, it built its nest on top of the ruby. The majestic creature paid no attention to the enraged shrieking from the back of the cave, where even more white-hot sparks were escaping through the crystal wall.

"Hurry! Oh, do hurry!" Demon said, clutching Peleus's hand without even noticing. "Oh, why doesn't it sing? What if the queen's medicine doesn't work?"

Peleus squeezed back. "It'll be all right," he said. "At least . . . I think it will. And we've got the other globe of nectar if we need to give it more."

Soon the nest was finished. It was square and perfect, laced with berries, fruit, bark, and flowers, which added flashes of color. The phoenix settled itself on top and opened its beak. For a breathless moment everything was still. Demon crossed every finger and toe he had.

Then a note of diamond-pure sound erupted from the phoenix's long beak, followed by another, and another, dropping like tiny jewels through the sulfur-laden air. The Song of Renewal was so beautiful that forever afterward both Demon and Peleus always compared it to each piece of music they heard. Nothing ever came close to the wonder of the phoenix's song.

The fire devils were not so happy with it, though. They cowered back, wailing high and shrill. Gradually, the cracks filled in and disappeared, and the crystal became less and less transparent. Soon it was so thick that no trace or sound of the fire devils could be seen or heard. They were safely trapped in their crystal prison for another hundred years, but still the phoenix sang.

Wisps of smoke began to rise from the wooden nest, and then flames followed.

"No!" Demon gasped, lurching forward. But Antaeus pulled him back with one ham-like hand.

"Hush!" he said. "This must happen. Wait and see."

As the giant spoke, the nest blazed up in a tall white pillar of fire. A delightful scent of cinnamon, frankincense, and rose replaced the sulfur smell. Then, as suddenly as it had appeared, the column of flame was gone—and the phoenix with it. The top of the ruby was completely empty apart from a mass of fluttering phoenix feathers, drifting through the air, and a large sapphire-and-gold egg that began to rock back and forth.

Soon small cracks appeared in the shell, and Demon could hear a tapping sound.

"It's going to hatch," said Peleus, rushing forward and dragging Demon behind him. "Look!"

The egg burst open in a shower of jagged blue-gold pieces, revealing a small golden chick that cheeped loudly. Before their astonished eyes, it grew and grew, until a full-size phoenix stood before them again, tail trailing magnificently down the side of the ruby, and crest raised high.

"Ah!" it said, in a beautifully musical voice. "That's more like it. It's always so cramped in my egg."

"Are you all right?" Demon asked. He still couldn't quite believe they'd succeeded.

"Better than new," it replied. "Thank you for curing me, Pandemonius—and you, too, young prince. I didn't think you'd make it back in time."

"We nearly didn't," said Demon. "Luckily, Antaeus is fast."

The phoenix cocked its head. "I suppose you'll

want more of my feathers for that cloak of yours, giant?" it said.

Antaeus nodded. "Someone . . ." He gave a sideways look at Demon. "Someone pulled a whole lot out."

Demon spluttered in protest. "I was only trying to help," he said. Antaeus just gave his great rumbling laugh and ruffled Demon's hair.

The phoenix fluttered down and picked up two feathers in its beak, then gave one each to Demon and Peleus.

"To thank you," it said. "Those few who belong to the Legion of Phoenix Protectors can call on me if they are ever in great need or danger, and I will come. Just throw the feather into a fire made of sandalwood and say my name. Remember, though, it only works once."

It nudged Demon's leg. "Take that globe of ant nectar with you, too," it said. "It might come in handy one day. It is powerful stuff. You'll know when to use it, I expect."

With that, it stretched out its wings and soared out through the firefall with a melodious cry of farewell.

Demon repacked his medicine sack, tucking the phoenix feather carefully inside Chiron's Book of Cures. "I suppose we'd better start getting back," he said sleepily. He was tired, and hungrier than a starving Chimera.

Demon woke from a deep sleep on Antaeus's shoulder when they reached the bottom of the mountain. As he opened his eyes, he saw Keith and Sky Pearl frolicking around a familiar tall figure with an owl on her shoulder. The goddess of wisdom smiled a knowing smile as she heard the sound of three rumbling stomachs coming toward her. She snapped her fingers, and on the flowers at her feet there appeared a magnificent picnic, spread on a cloth of silver-embroidered purple. Demon's mouth began to water, and he had to swallow hard to keep from dribbling.

"Well done, Pandemonius," Athena said, drawing him aside from the others as they fell on the food like starving wolves. "Before you eat, I have a reward for you. A certain owl told me you'd like it." As Sophie hooted softly, the goddess reached into the air and drew out a beautiful book, bound in red leather and gold. Demon's eyes grew as round as apples as he took it and opened it. It was full of creamy-white blank pages.

"Oh," he said, stroking its smoothness. "It's so much better than my old slate! Now I can write my patient notes just like Chiron does."

Athena laughed. "I suggest you start with the case of the poorly phoenix," she said.

"I shall, Your Cleverness," he replied as she and

Sophie disappeared in a flash of silver light.

"Hey, Demon," said Peleus. "Come and eat before Antaeus snaffles these honey cakes."

"Hands off!" said Demon happily. "Those are all mine!"

GLOSSARY

PRONUNCIATION GUIDE

THE GODS

Aphrodite (AF-ruh-DY-tee): Goddess of love and beauty and all things pink and fluffy.

Apollo (uh-POL-oh): The radiant god of music. More than a little sensitive to criticism.

Artemis (AR-te-miss): Goddess of the hunt. Can't decide if she wants to protect animals or kill them.

Athena (a-THEE-na): Goddess of wisdom and defender of pesky, troublesome heroes.

Chiron (KY-ron): God of the centaurs. Known for his wisdom and healing abilities.

Dionysus (DY-uh-NY-suss): God of wine. Turns even sensible gods into silly goons.

Eos (EE-oss): The Titan goddess of the dawn. Makes things rosy with a simple touch of her fingers.

Eros (AIR-oss): The rascally, winged god of love.

Hades (HAY-deez): Zeus's brother, the gloomy, fearsome ruler of the Underworld.

Helios (HEE-lee-us): The bright, shiny, and blinding Titan god of the sun.

Hephaestus (Hih-FESS-tuss): God of blacksmithing, metalworking, fire, volcanoes, and most things awesome.

Hera (HEER-a): Zeus's scary wife. Drives a chariot pulled by screechy peacocks.

Hermes (HUR-meez): The clever, fun-loving, jack-of-all-trades messenger god.

Hestia (HESS-tee-ah): Goddess of the hearth and home. Bakes the most heavenly treats.

Pan (PAN): God of shepherds and flocks. Frequently found wandering grassy hillsides, playing his pipes.

Poseidon (puh-SY-dun): God of the sea and controller of natural and supernatural events.

Zeus (ZOOSS): King of the gods. Fond of smiting people with lightning bolts.

OTHER MYTHICAL BEINGS

Antaeus (ahn-TAY-oos): Giant who likes to challenge everyone he meets to a fight.

Asclepius (as-KLEE-pee-us): Born the half-god son of Apollo, but raised by Chiron the centaur as an apprentice. Doctors love him.

Autolykos (ow-TOL-ih-kohs): A trickster who shape-shifts his stolen goods to avoid getting caught.

Dryads (DRY-ads): Tree nymphs. Can literally sing trees to life.

Endeis (en-DEE-es): Never a dull moment when you're the daughter of Chiron, mother of Peleus, and official oread of Mount Pelion.

Heracles (HAIR-a-kleez): The half-god "hero" who just *loooves* killing magical beasts.

Myrmidons (MER-muh-donz): Zeus transformed this lean, mean, fighting colony of ants into human soldiers.

Nymphs (NIMFS): Giggly, girly, dancing nature spirits.

Oreads (OR-ee-adz): Nymphs that play in the mountains and hills.

Peleus (PEE-lee-us): A hero and the prince of the ant-men. Relies a little too much on his magical sword.

Prometheus (pruh-MEE-thee-us): Gave fire to mankind and was sentenced to eternal torture by bird-pecking.

PLACES

Aegina (ee-JYE-nuh): Island near Athens ruled by Peleus's father. Home of the ant-men.

Mount Pelion (PEEL-ee-un): A mountain in the Aegean Sea where Chiron the centaur lives.

BEASTS

Centaur (SEN-tor): Half man, half horse, and lucky enough to get the best parts of both.

Colchian Dragon (KOL-kee-un): Ares's guard dragon. Has magical teeth and supposedly never sleeps.

Griffin (GRIH-fin): Couldn't decide if it was better to be a lion or an eagle, so decided to be both.

Hydra (HY-druh): Nine-headed water serpent. Hera somehow finds this lovable.

Phoenix (FEE-nix): Wondrous bird with a burning desire to be reborn every hundred years.

ABOUT THE AUTHOR

Lucy Coats studied English and ancient history at Edinburgh University, then worked in children's publishing, and now writes full-time. She is a gifted children's poet and writes for all ages from two to teenage. She is widely respected for her lively retellings of myths. Her twelve-book series Greek Beasts and Heroes was published by Orion in the UK. Beasts of Olympus is her first US chapter-book series. Lucy's website is www.lucycoats.com. You can also follow her on Twitter @lucycoats.

ABOUT THE ILLUSTRATOR

As a kid, **Brett Bean** made stuff up to get out of trouble. As an adult, Brett makes stuff up to make people happy. Brett creates art for film, TV, games, books, and toys. He works on his tan and artwork in California with his wife, Julie Anne, and son, Finnegan Hobbes. He hopes to leave the world a little bit better for having him. You can find more about Brett and his artwork at www.2dbean.com.